Many Happy Returns

For Trevor, Lucy and family

First published in Great Britain by
HarperCollins Publishers Ltd in 1994
First published in Picture Lions in 1995
Picture Lions is an imprint of the Children's Division,
part of HarperCollins Publishers Ltd
Copyright © Mark Burgess 1994
A CIP catalogue record for this title
is available from the British Library.
The author asserts the moral right
to be identified as the author of the work.
ISBN: 0 00 664547 X
Printed and bound in Hong Kong

Many Happy Returns

MARK BURGESS

PictureLions

An Imprint of HarperCollins*Publishers*

INTRODUCTION

A few years ago Hannah Hedgehog took over the little hotel by the sea from her Aunt Hetty. Hannah's aunt was tired of hotel life and had decided to travel the world in her hot air balloon.

These days Hannah's Hotel is the ideal place for a holiday. Hannah is helped by Molly Mouse; Sam Squirrel is the cook and Rodney Rabbit does all the odd jobs.

Everything is done to make the visitors happy. However, sometimes things don't go quite according to plan – such as when the tortoises had their special party.

"What a lovely cake, Sam," said Hannah. It was a chocolate cake, Hannah's favourite and Sam had made it for the special party being held at Hannah's Hotel that day. It was Old Toby Tortoise's hundredth birthday and all his relations were coming to the hotel to celebrate. "I think they've arrived," called Molly from the dining room where she was laying the tables.

She could see
cars parking by the
boathouse on the mainland.
"What, already? They're very early," said
Hannah. "I'll go and tell Rodney to fetch them
in the ferryboat. The tide's in, so they can't
walk across."

"Perhaps I'd better put the lunch on," said
Sam to himself and he began to check through
his list of food.

Hannah found Rodney in the garden. He was
watering his lettuces.
"Look at those, have
you ever seen such
beautiful lettuces?"
said Rodney, proudly.
"Yes, they're lovely
Rodney," said Hannah. "I came to tell you that
the tortoises have arrived."
"What, already? But it's only eleven o'clock!
Oh well, I suppose I'd better go and fetch
them."
"Yes, please, Rodney," said Hannah.

When Rodney arrived at the mainland the tortoises were still getting out of their cars. "Hello," said Cecil Tortoise, who had organized the party. "I think we're all here. Martha, hurry up, there's a dear. We don't want to be late. Now then, be careful getting into the boat everybody. Nigel, let Old Toby go first."

"I'm a hundred years old today, but I don't feel it," said Old Toby Tortoise. "These are my relations, from all over the world, you know."

"Congratulations," said Rodney. "What a large family. We might have to make two trips. Please remain seated during the crossing."

"Nigel, sit down," said Cecil Tortoise. "Didn't you hear?"

It took quite some time to get everybody into the ferryboat. It was a bit of a squeeze. They were all just getting comfortable when Martha Tortoise realized that she'd left her spectacles in her car so she had to get out again.

And then two of the little tortoises said they felt sea sick before Rodney had even started the engine. But at last everybody was settled and they crossed to the island.

When the tortoises eventually reached the
hotel, Hannah was at the front door to meet
them. It was well past lunchtime.

"Hello," said Cecil Tortoise,
"I hope we're not late."
He was a bit short of
breath after walking
up from the beach.

"I'm a hundred years old today," said Old Toby
Tortoise as he struggled up the steps. "But,
you know, I don't feel a hundred."

"He doesn't look it, either,"
said Martha Tortoise.

"Congratulations," said Hannah. "Now as
lunch is ready, I'll show you all
straight into the dining room
and then you can look round
the hotel afterwards."

In the dining room Hannah
and Molly handed round
the menus and then waited
to take the orders.
Everybody watched as
Old Toby Tortoise tried
to make up his mind.
"I think I'll just have
a little lettuce," he said.
"But lettuce isn't on the
menu," said Molly.
"Oh," said Old Toby.
"It's all right, there is
lettuce," said Hannah.
"Ooo, lettuce would be
lovely," said Martha Tortoise.
"I want lettuce," said Nigel,
banging his fork on the table.

Everybody wanted lettuce.

Sam was upset.
Nobody wanted
his watercress soup.
Nobody wanted his
asparagus mousse.
Nobody wanted anything he'd made. They
just wanted lettuces. Ordinary, dull lettuces.

"I said there should have been lettuces on the
menu," said Rodney when Hannah asked
for some. "Ten, twenty –
take what you need.
You won't taste
better lettuces
than those."

Rodney wasn't quite so
pleased when Hannah
asked for another twenty-five
lettuces a little later. The tortoises
wanted lettuce for pudding. Sam made some
green custard to go with it.

"Hannah," said Sam. "They're not going to
want that chocolate cake I made are they?"
"Probably not, Sam," said Hannah, cheerfully.
"But never mind. Make one
out of lettuces instead."

Sam started to
think about that.

"Now then," said Cecil Tortoise, when lunch was finished. "Everybody line up for the photograph. Over here, Martha, I think." Cecil busied himself setting up his tripod and camera.

"But you won't be in the picture," said Martha. "Yes I will," said Cecil. "If I press this button I can run round to that space there before the camera takes the picture."

Unfortunately the camera took the picture
before Cecil was in his place. He couldn't run
quite fast enough. They would have to ask
somebody else to take the picture.
Cecil caught sight of Rodney
but he looked rather grumpy
and disappeared into the greenhouse.
Then Dora Dormouse came into the garden.

"Oh, how interesting," said Dora.
"A Snapikki CU4T. A really excellent camera.
What? You'd like me to take a picture?
Oh, thank you. Yes, now let me see.
Did you want all those tortoises
in the picture or just the hotel?"

After Dora had taken the photograph the whole party sat enjoying the sun. Some of the younger tortoises paddled in the swimming pool.

About tea-time, Molly noticed that Old Toby Tortoise seemed to be looking for something on the mainland.

"What can it be?" she asked Hannah.
"I don't know," said Hannah. "But now they're
all looking."

Then Cecil Tortoise came up to them. He was
very worried. "It hasn't arrived," he said.
"Surely the telegram should
have arrived by now."
"Of course, the telegram!"
said Hannah. "From the
Palace, congratulating
Old Toby Tortoise
on his hundredth birthday.
Don't worry, I'll telephone
and find out what's happened."
"Oh, thank you, thank you," said Cecil.

Hannah dialled the number.
"Oh, hello, is that
the Palace?" she said
and explained about
the telegram.
"Just a minute, please,"
said the voice at the Palace.
Hannah waited. "Yes," said the voice, "we are
very sorry but according to our records,
Toby Tortoise is only ninety-nine."

"Oh dear," said Hannah
when she had put down the receiver.
"What is it?" said Cecil Tortoise, anxiously.

"He's only ninety-nine," said Hannah.
Cecil Tortoise went white as a sheet.
"B-B-B-B-but what are we going
to do?" he stammered.
"Old Toby will be so
disappointed."

They all thought for a bit.

"We could make up a telegram,"
suggested Molly.
"Could we?" said Cecil.
"Why not?" said Hannah. "I'll do it. Molly,
serve tea with the birthday cake and then we
can pretend the telegram arrived when they
weren't looking."

"Oh yes, thank you,"
said Cecil Tortoise,
getting his colour back.

Sam was proud of his birthday cake.
He'd used the last of Rodney's lettuces, tied
together with red ribbon and lots of candles
on top. Molly lighted the candles and carried
the cake into the garden.

"Ooo!" said all the tortoises when they saw it.

Everybody sang 'Happy Birthday' and then
Old Toby Tortoise tried to
blow out the candles,
but he had a lot of trouble.
Molly had bought the sort that
keep re-lighting. Old Toby thought it was
very funny and could hardly stop giggling.

"A telegram has arrived!" said Hannah,
flourishing a bit of paper.

"Oh, we didn't see it arrive!" said the tortoises.
"It's from the Palace."
"Hush, please, everybody," said Cecil Tortoise.
"Nigel, be quiet."

Hannah read from
the piece of paper.
*"Her Majesty sends greetings and
congratulations to Toby Tortoise on the
occasion of his one hundredth birthday.
Many Happy Returns!"*

"Stuff and nonsense," said a voice from behind her. "Hello Toby, remember me? Tina Gerbil, from the maths class, just popped by to wish you Happy 99th Birthday. Not 100, Toby, 99. You must have got your sums wrong – again."
All the tortoises gasped.

Everybody was quiet.
They all looked at Old Toby Tortoise.

He was busy counting.
Then he began to
giggle again.
Then laugh and laugh
and then his deckchair collapsed.
Everybody rushed to help him.

"Eaten too many lettuces, I shouldn't wonder,"
said Rodney.
"It's all right," said Old Toby Tortoise,
still giggling. "We'll just have to have
another party next year."

Hannah was in a bit of a daze.
"Gerbils..." she muttered. "Gerbils... Oh no!"
And she rushed to the kitchen.

But she was too late.
Tina Gerbil's family was just finishing the last
of the chocolate cake.

Here are some more Picture Lions

BADGER'S PARTING GIFTS
Susan Varley

Quentin Blake
MISTER MAGNOLIA

KATIE MORAG AND THE TIRESOME TED
Mairi Hedderwick

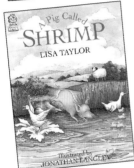

A Pig Called SHRIMP
LISA TAYLOR
Illustrated by JONATHAN LANGLEY

A BAD WEEK FOR The THREE BEARS
TONY BRADMAN & JENNY WILLIAMS

Reckless Ruby
by Hiawyn Oram
Illustrated by Tony Ross

Monsters
Colin & Jacqui Hawkins

WHERE THE WILD THINGS ARE
STORY AND PICTURES BY MAURICE SENDAK

Michael Rosen & Quentin Blake
DON'T Put Mustard in the Custard

for you to enjoy